Kate Vannah

From heart to heart

Kate Vannah

From heart to heart

ISBN/EAN: 9783744736541

Printed in Europe, USA, Canada, Australia, Japan

Cover: Foto ©Andreas Hilbeck / pixelio.de

More available books at **www.hansebooks.com**

FROM HEART TO HEART.

BY

KATE VANNAH,

AUTHOR OF "VERSES."

There are four or five who in passing this place
While they live will name me yet ;
And when I am gone will think on my face,
And feel a kind of regret.

JEAN INGELOW.

WITH PORTRAIT.

BOSTON

J. G. CUPPLES COMPANY,

250 BOYLSTON STREET.

Sincerely Yours,
Kate Sanmah

Dedicated to

CHARLOTTE FREDRIKA KENNAN.

How, Dearest, wilt thou have me for most use?
A hope, to sing by gladly? or a fine,
Sad memory, with thy songs to interfuse?
A shade, in which to sing—of palm, or pine?
A grave, on which to rest from singing? Choose.

ELIZABETH BARRETT BROWNING.

CONTENTS.

CONTENTS.

CONTENTS.

FROM HEART TO HEART.

SONNETS.

I.

" Can I make white enough my thought for thee,
Or wash my words in light? "

Love, lower thine eyes.   They are too reverent.   Sink
   Me to the lowest level thou can'st find
   In thy deep nature.   That will seem more kind
To both.   Some day thou'lt thank me.   Learn to think
Of me a beggar, fit not e'en to drink
   The love upon thy lips.   Thou art so blind
   To his unworthiness whom thou dost bind
Each hour closer by some golden link
Forged in thy woman's nature.   Rather learn
   To look down on me as in babyhood

My mother looked upon me ; all a-yearn,
  And prayerful that I might grow noble, good.
Sometimes e'en she, whose body and soul gave strength
    to me,
Now leans on him whose steps she watched so tremu-
  lously.

II.

FAME.

R. B. and E. B. B.

" There dwelt he happy; there that minstrel queen,
Who shared his poet crown, but gladdened more
To hold, unshared, her poet's manly heart."
                                        AUBREY DE VERE.

My heart's Belovëd !   To-night they talked of Fame.
  One cried, with gaze on me—" Say what it means :
  For when thou singest a whole world loving leans
To list thy heart's pulse in thy verse.   No blame
Can touch thee now.   Who would not change the name
  Of king for thine ? "
                                        I was 'mid quiet scenes
Alone with thee, from whom my man's heart gleans
  Perpetual inspiration.   O'er me came
A sudden shyness 'neath their waiting eyes,
  And I was dumb.
                                        I have come home—to thee.
I kneel beside thy couch while my soul cries
  For gladness to be here : " Enough for me
That one heart for my coming ever longs,
That one low, tender voice sings my poor songs."

(3)

BETROTHED.

"This new joy—half pain."

I BEAR my dear joy with unquiet heart
  In these first hours, Belovëd.   Give me space
  To still these leaping pulses—hide my face
Until my lips be firmer.   How I start
And flush from hand to brow, and swiftly dart
  A frightened glance around, if from thy place
  Thou look'st my way, or, with that flexile grace
None other hath, thou risest to depart,
  To leave me lonelier in a crowded room
  Than hunted exile 'mid the forest's gloom.
It is too soon to realize thou art mine—
Though I so long, Belovëd, have been thine.
  Last night an envied rose lay on thy breast
  Where soon, so soon, my happy head may rest.

FIRST LOVE.

"For God in cursing gives us better gifts
Than men in benediction."
AURORA LEIGH.

A HUMAN friend was granted unto me,
And I, bewildered by my sweet, strange love,
With eyes on earth, forgot that from above
My blessing came.   Blinded, I would not see
God's image in my friend.   Each came to be
The other's god.   Nor future, nor the past
We heeded.   We forgot that death came last.
Men call this Love : 'tis but idolatry.

My lover looked within my eyes and swore,
"No power on earth, nor yet in heaven should take
My love from him.   If I at first the shore
Of dread eternity should gain, he'd break
God's law, and take his life to share my fate."
One heard, Who mercifully changed our love to hate.

(5)

V.

LAST LOVE.

"I take you, and thank God!"

R. B.

Lo! here I stand all trembling and dismayed
   Within the still, sweet garden of thy heart.
O Love! all is so white, I feel afraid
   To stir, or speak, or breathe.   No more to part
In life or death. . . . I dare to lift my eyes,
   And feast them on the fragrant flowers here.
Pure as thou art, within me wakes surprise
   That in this hour immortal should appear
No vivid blooms; though blushes come and go
   Upon thy face,—while, 'neath thy half-closed lids,
Flash changing lights,—the red lips tremble so;
   Fain thou would'st speak, yet sweet confusion bids
Thy voice be silent. . . God! this is the goal
Next heaven.   Let me not cast Sin's shadow o'er this soul.

(6)

VI.

BY THE SEA.

Last year I knew naught of thee save thy name,
Of love my life seemed full as it could hold.
Not by one word of warning was I told
Thy royal advent. Life's face looked the same
As it had looked for years, when swift there came
Her King.
                Cor Cordium ! how was I to know
A rich red rose would leap forth from the snow
To startle, and to blind me with the flame
Of its wild beauty ? See, the white gull dips
Her breast unto the ocean's murmuring lips ;
And see upon its bosom the great ships :
They only know the surface of the sea
Not dreaming of its depths. Love, none knew me——
I did not know myself 'till I loved thee.

(7)

COMPENSATED.

WERE God to strike me blind until the day
My lids unclose to show my trembling soul
Beneath His Eyes—Belovëd, I would say:
" I was content to stumble to the goal
Through darkened years, once having seen a face
That glowed, a lamp eternal, at the end
Of Life's dark corridor."

With a like grace,
Submissive to His will, so would I bend
My soul in mute acceptance should I miss
All sense of sound, once having heard a voice
That fed my spirit's hearing with a bliss
Perpetual : e'en as the shells rejoice,
Leagues inland borne, to murmur of the sea
Whose voice lives in their depths eternally.

(8)

HURT.

DEAR God ! The friend whom I love best, to-day—
(The best of all), such cruel words did say
That I at first felt all benumbed—then sore,—
Then hopeless grew my heart lest nevermore
Its pain should cease.   Our day had just begun.
The earth laughed in Thy light,—when swift, the sun
Did fail to warm me.

               Oh ! When I am dead
Will death be colder than the words he said
In bitterness, in scorn, e'en unbelief
Of me who loved him ?   Stricken mute by Grief
I stole away.   No eyes have seen my face
Till now.   I'm kneeling here to beg the grace
Of penitence for sins that give Thee pain
Like this.   Christ, let me wound Thee ne'er again !

ON THE CHASM'S BRINK.

I LIE along this rocky bed, and peer
Into the chasm deep where waters rush
And rage with hungry roar which God could hush
With just a thought.

     I cannot even hear
Thy matchless voice, for all thou art so near ;
Yet I may have thine eyes, and the soft touch
Of thy firm hands that mean to me as much
As others' speech. And in thine eyes so clear
E'en is enough to satisfy my sight.

Some one has leaped across to that smooth stone
Out there—mid-torrent,—scornful he of fright—
To carve upon its face his name alone :
Dost thou remember, Love, my daring leap
To write upon thy heart one name so deep ?

X.

A JACQUEMINOT.

I SINGLE from rich clusters one great rose
And give it one long kiss.   A thing more fair
In all the world there is not save the rare
Rose in thy bosom beating !
              See, it grows
Impatient for thine eyes although it knows
With what a dangerous rival 't must compare.
Its petals part, its fragrant heart lies bare
To die in rapture on thine own held close.
I kiss it now.   The pleasance and the pain,
The ecstasy thy love hath brought to me ;
The hunger for thy heart to rest again
On mine through time—yea—through Eternity,
The loneliness of life because I miss
Thee, Love—are all concentred in this kiss.

(11)

WITH THEE AGAIN.

"The silence of life more pathetic than death's!"

E. B. B.

WAS it then Pride that all this lonely year
  Did hold my lips from any speech with thee?
  And was it Pride that would not let me see
That face that I so loved, nor let me hear
Thy voice that last fell coldly on mine ear?
  (This memory alone is agony).
Love had so often made me bend my knee
When blameless for thy pardon; that a fear
Which seemed to melt my courage all away,
Did seize and haunt me, lest thou should'st one day
  Lose thy respect for one less strong than thee.
  So, Dear, we parted. We! and cruelly.
Now do I know 'twas Pride did make me wait.
Not blameless, once again, Dear Heart, I kneel—too late.

IN A CATHEDRAL.

To-night, at sunset hour, I stole away,
  And wandered to the vast Cathedral's door,
Entering which, I thought : The soiled hand of the poor,
  E'en as the hand of proud patrician, may
Swing the great doors. Here all may come to pray.
  The beggar's naked feet may tread the floor
By jeweled robes of king or queen swept o'er.
  Believers, doubters, outcasts—murderers—lay
Their souls' most deadly secrets open here
  Behind those crimson folds, and know not fear.

Under the lamp a beggar knelt in prayer.
The sinking sun looked through a window rare,
And painted rags in colors of royalty :
E'en so thy great love glorifieth me !

(13)

XIII.

"WEDDED."

(By Sir Frederic Leighton.)

COUNTING the world for love well lost, apart
From every soul they stand.
       Heart known to heart,
As yet they feel no need to speak one word.
Only the great Sea's solemn voice is heard
In war eternal with those massive walls.
Adown her lifted face the sunlight falls—
Less blinding than the light in his dear eyes
She so doth love ; that with delight, surprise,
And joy too keen, her lover, leonine,
Shivers to think, "till death—yea ! after—mine."
His eyes are closed. Her left hand's finger-tips
Are reverently pressed against his lips
That move at last. And see ! the woman's life
Stands still to listen while he breathes, " My wife ! "

HELEN HUNT JACKSON. HARRIET BEECHER STOWE, AND JULIA WARD HOWE.

ONE in her lonely mountain-grave lies sleeping
Where silvery waters laugh through all the year,
As if in joyaunce ever to sing near
Her who so loved them while her soul was weeping
O'er wrongs whose righting God gave to her keeping.
Another, with a heart that knew not fear,
Dealt Slavery's chain a blow so loud and clear,
That millions heard its music with hearts leaping:
As millions bless the day she saw the light,
So millions must lament her when she dies. . . . .
The third but lifts her gentle voice, and hies
The thinking world to wonder at the might
Of masculine mind close-wed to woman's heart.
She has her throne above our womankind—apart.

1885.

(15)

A SNOWLESS DECEMBER DAY AT THE NORTH.

ENCHANTED, here I linger on the hill,
  And look across the river at my feet.
The king o' the White Heart hath deemed it meet
Not to assume his ermine robes until
He bids farewell to Autumn, to him still
  A queen, though crownless !
                    He would fain entreat
One smile ere burying her in snow and sleet.
His captive late so fair, he grieves to kill.

Down in the glen I see a bit of green—
A fern that would be leal unto the queen.
Winter meant well, I doubt not, when he blew
Last night one freezing breath across the river,
And made a mirror, clear, for her to view
Her faded face—no worse blow could he give her !

(16)

GOOD FRIDAY.

(3 o'c.)

CHRIST! see me, hear me in this awful hour!
Face-down, upon the altar steps I lie.
The lamp is out, no living creature nigh.
Soul-sick at being so long within the power
Of Sin ; I leap from his embrace to cower
Here, at Thy wounded feet.

       Oh ! hear my cry—
" In this, the hour Thou'st died. let me, too, die ! "
Perfect repentance, only, is my dower.
Tired of trying to gain omniscience over
Poor human hearts that change from day to day ;
Sick of the fickle worldling for a lover—
Here, at Thy feet. forever let me stay.
Let my great love like healing ointment cover
Thy wounds from which my eyes no more shall stray.

RECONCILED.

In no more fitting place could we have met,
At no more fitting time, a wailing night.
We, who for years have shunned each other's sight,
Who strove to bury Love beyond Regret,
Who begged of God the power to forget
Each other's eyes, voice, lips :—who did so blight
And bruise each other's hearts with all Pride's might.

Just the dead body of our friend—warm yet—
Divides us. . . We could feel each other's breath
Should one lean low to scan the patient face
Of her who pleaded so before her death
For us to be at peace. . . . . See, Love ! I place
My hand near yours. . . . . .
                            You clasp, and hold it fast !
Such tears as wet her dead face drown our past.

(18)

TWICE PARTED.

"And thou, clock, striking the hour's pulses on,
Chime in the day that ends these parting days !"

E. B. B.

ONCE, in the storm, we said good-bye.   I stayed
And watched you sail beneath a sullen sky.
Quivering with pain, I moaned : " Belovëd, good-bye ! "
You could not hear, but you looked long, and laid
Your hands against your lips and heart.

Afraid
I only was whilst parted you might die,
And not beside me in the same grave lie.
But God returned you. . . .   Not to me.   You strayed
Since then beyond my reach while yet in sight.
With eyes upon my face you see me not.
Oh ! had you sunk into the sea that night—
Then ! when you loved me, ere you had forgot—
Then ! when of all God's world you loved but me,
Widowed my life—your love mine for Eternity !

XIX.

PRESENTIMENT.

" Oh, clasp we to our hearts for deathless dower,
This close-companioned, inarticulate hour ! "

DANTE ROSSETTI.

HOLD close my trembling hands against thy heart
Oh, thou, my Life ! whom yearning did compel
To come again in thrilling voice to tell
So much of love as poor words may impart.
And 'gainst mine lay thy face.   Until we part
Let me be near thee.   Speak or silent be.
The love of my whole waiting life to thee
I give—and would give more.   Quick tears do start
'Mid rapture, e'en to think how cruelly brief
Is bliss like this—how long the after grief.
A half year since, that nest now filled with snow
Brimmed o'er with love and music.

This will go—

Our wondrous moment.   Close enfold thou me—
When nests are warm again one heart may frozen be.

(20)

XX.

FRONTING ETERNITY.

*"How could I let thee stray
Into the vale of death, thy torch unlit,
And mine ablaze that might have kindled it ?
Oh, what befell thee on that fearsome way ?
And oh, what greeting would be thine to me
Could thy voice reach me from eternity ?"*

K. E. C.

ONE whispers : " He will die now, soon." Straightway
My whole life's volume meets my dying gaze—
Just for an instant—ere flesh turns to clay.
Across one page a blinding white light plays
To show me where I grievously did sin
Against a woman's soul, as white and pure
As lilies in God's garden. I to win
Her heart was not content, and I did lure
Her soul away from Thee, my God ! from Thee.

Long years ago that soul went to receive
Its final judgment. Does she now for me
Forgiveness plead ? Was she denied reprieve—
She who repented so ? Is she in heaven ?
What if at last, through her, I be forgiven !

(21)

"THE THIRD THE CHARM IS."

THE first day that your letter failed me, Dear,
  I felt surprise, yet said, "She's occupied,
  And, save sweet thoughts, could spare me naught
    beside ;
To-morrow morn her letter will be here."
Morn came, no letter bringing, then a fear
  And—yes—a tear ; yet still I bravely tried
  To look at least as though you had not died !
But all that day my eyes were not quite clear

Another day, the third. "Now surely she
  My anxious heart will pacify to-day,
And in her tender letter I shall see
  Regret for this unusual delay."
But no. I knelt and prayed, oppressed by fear,
And, rising from my knees, beheld you—here !

(22)

WEDDED LOVERS.

*" When first thine earnest eyes with mine were crossed,
And love called love."*

FIVE years to-night, my Life's Own, since thy face
  My glad eyes found, to love as soon as seen.
  But briefly 'tween our spirits stood that screen
We raise to hide from stranger eyes all trace
Of what most sacred is within that place
  Close-sentineled from curious eyes and keen :
  The soul's still sanctuary,—oft closed e'en
To those whose presence lends a tender grace
  Unto our daily lives.
                        I heard thy voice,
And trembled to its diapason tone.
  Like very children how did we rejoice
That first day that we fled the world, alone.
  The joy, ineffable, comes back to me
I felt when thy dear lips met mine so tenderly.

(23)

DEVOTION.

Thou who art far from me, Belovëd, hear
My deepest thought. I wish that it might be
That thou could'st open wide my heart and see
In one immortal glance, swift, deep, and clear,
How I own nothing there ; nor smile, nor tear,
Nor wish, nor thought have separate from thee.
The yearning years, O Love, are long to me.
Her little one no mother holds more dear
Than I my life since thou hast called me thine ;
Guards not her eyes more faithfully than mine
Are guarded. Love ! God's angels all might know
My thoughts by night and day the while I go
My watchful way, as on my breast were sleeping
A little child left to my tender keeping.

XXIV.

LOVE'S MIRACLE.

" Our hands would touch for all the mountain-bars."

E. B. B.

I HAVE you in the heart of me for aye.
I hold you here. A thousand leagues away,
   You move through scenes that I shall never know—
   Save that you carry me where'er you go.
All that delights you sinks into your heart
Where I await you 'till the rest depart.
   Oh ! mystery of mutual love.   I hold
   You fast within my heart.   When we enfold
Each other, Love, some happy hour now far
Away as gleams to-night the farthest star,
   I shall not have you nearer.

                    Yonder stands
The organ, silent.   It but waits my hands
   To wake its voice, and kiss the silence deep—
   So love doth wait your coming, in my heart, asleep.

(25)

XXV.

IN THE LONELY NIGHT.

"I say with sobbing breath the old fond prayer."

"God bless thee, my Belovëd, and good-night " . . .
With thee so far away, more fervently
E'en than of old I breathe the prayer for thee;
More humbly now than when I had the light
Of actual presence, and the happy right
To lean and kiss thy face.   Then thou to me;
While on thy forehead, pure, all reverently
I traced a sign that gives to weakness might,
That banishes all evil thoughts, and brings
The peace of God.   Sign of the sufferings
Immortal, that were Christ's: sign of His cross.
Dear sign ! that after loneliness and loss,
We yet shall walk together in God's sight—
"God bless thee, my Belovëd, and good-night !"

(26)

MUTATION.

HEIGHO ! the moods you have been in to-day
Would put to shame mad March or April weather.
One moment you would take my breath away,
Ineffably enchanting me.   Together
We scarce had been an hour by the Sea
(As high above it as the eagle's nest ·
Hangs o'er men's heads); you had tormented me
A score of times, until my aching breast
Heaved like the Sea.

                  Then seeing what discontent,
What pain and restlessness you could evoke ;
With blinding fascination swift you leant
Above me, low and lower—and you spoke,
Three words so musically that all sorrow
Vanished——(She speaks)—" I'll bring it back
    to-morrow ! "

SELF-CONQUERED.

Go, if thou wilt, Belovëd, far from me,
What way soever Pleasure beckons thee,
But make this heart thy refuge still, alway.
The key is thine—no other's—stray or stay.
When thou art wearied, in that chamber rest.
When thou art grieved, and deemest quiet best ;
When thou art sad, or glad, my tenderness
Shall shield thy moods of silence.   None shall guess
Thy presence there.   Alas ! what breaks my voice ?
Three times I tried to say : " E'en bring thy choice
Of one alone whose presence is most sweet,
And I that friend with gracious word will greet."
Forgive, Love ! that I faltered . . . .   " Yea ! " I cry :
" Bring e'en that friend thou lovest—though I die ! "

XXVIII.

SONNET.

HIS CONFESSION.

I CANNOT die, and not confess to thee—
Loved still—how once I shamed Love's loyalty.
   True love is love in truth forever, though
   She craves years to recover from the blow
Desertion deals.   It was in those first days.
When Love's too sorely bruised, Love often says
   In her delirium things she could not mean.
   Upon my knees I prayed (I must not screen
One fault in this last message), I did pray
Through many a lonely night, and lonely day,
   That : *long and bitter as each hour to me ;*
   So long, so hard, each year might be to thee !
   Now, ever in the lonely night I cry :
   " God ! let me bear her sufferings 'till I die ! "

(29)

SONNET.

CHALLENGED.

Nay, nay,—thy doubt offends Love's majesty—
  Strikes at the very root of Peace and Joy.
A dagger in my heart where, yesterday,
  Peace crooned, and sang in bliss, without alloy.
Look back, adown the dangerful, steep ways
  We climbed to gain these cool, still, beauteous
    heights.
E'en with her past unveiled, Love ne'er betrays
  Her chosen One, whom she alone invites
Unto the highest realms she may attain
  This side of heaven. . . .
                    Here, fling my head far back,—
Thy palm against my forehead—so. Now strain
  Thy sight its uttermost along the track
My soul, my heart, my thoughts have coursed for years.
Be not afraid : Truth, smiling, waits behind these tears.

(30)

LOOKING BACK.

FAR back as Memory's eyes can see to-night,
  Along the path that leads to womanhood,
  They can discern no day so fair and good
As that on which your face dawned on my sight.
The added joys of years cannot delight
  My soul as did that hour's. You spoke, and, lo!
  My heart was satisfied, nor cared to go
Beyond your reach,—never seemed life so bright.

I look once more. Far as my blinded eyes
  Can reach, I see no day one-half so drear
  As when I called you, and you could not hear
For distance and for waves that drowned my cries:
  If you should come, and call me thus in vain,
  Know that my love grew stronger for that pain.

REFUGE.

As in a storm, to some sweet chapel, calm,
  I hie from wild winds and the lightning's glare,
  And feel secure while bending there in prayer
Low at the quiet altar, where no harm
Can enter in to mar the spirit's balm,
  Where, hiding from the world, I weep, and dare
  My heart and soul beneath Christ's Face to bare,
Till on their quivering strings Peace plays her psalm;
  So, friend of mine, when thorns have pierced my
    heart,
And lava-tides of passion scorch my soul,
  In spirit do I hasten where thou art,
And, 'neath thy gentle voice, regain control
  Of my wild heart. Ah! shall the day dawn never
  When I may have thine actual presence ever?

FULL RECOGNITION.

ABOVE my desk there hangs a picture old,
  Whose age precise to no man now is known.
  I only know 'tis greater than my own
By years ; for, as a little child, I'm told,
I'd lie for hours and watch the twisted gold
    Of its rich frame.   Then, when I'd older grown,
    My interest on the picture dwelt alone,
Till now, of all my treasures, I do hold
This picture as the rarest.

                          So with thee :
Though thou wert fair to me that summer day,
  When to a lonely heart thou cam'st to be
Its blessing ; oh, Dear One, I cannot say
  How broad, how deep my need is of thee now.
  In my life's crown the rarest jewel thou !

XXXIII.

A FLOWER'S NAME.

Down in the tender grasses 'neath my sill,
  Where I lean forth each day to greet the dawn,
  And lean again when light from earth is gone
To pray for thee; all of its own sweet will,
  A tiny flower has come, so fair and still,
  And new to me, I've given it thy name.
So often do I marvel why it came
The evening air with redolence to fill.
  The first time that I found it blooming there,
  At once I cried, " God answers thus the prayer
Which every morn and every eve I say
For my soul's friend, so far, so far away.
  He yields this sign that, after our long pain
  Of separation, we shall meet again."

(34)

TO GEORGE ELIOT.

You tell of rapture felt by human hearts
    That wake when comes their hour of mutual love ;
    Your own has caught from the Great Heart above
A sympathy and love divine.   When starts
The mourner's bitter tear, and when departs
    From the worn way a once all spotless dove,
    God-like, you follow on and give your love,
Which must avail when fail all other arts.

Regretfully we lay your books aside,
    Feeling as though some glorious symphony
Which had ennobled life that moment died,
    Whose echo ne'er can die to memory.
E'en as old masters' music hath defied
    Oblivion, so your words must lasting be !
    1880

(35)

FOREBODING.

GIVE me assurance that your love will stay,
  And be my benediction through the year,
  At whose approach I tremble with a fear,
A terror, lest its hours should lead away
One heart from which my own could never stray.
  I'm sad as death to-night,--come closer, Dear,—
  My foolish heart is troubled ; let me hear
And feel assurance, my sad fears allay.
How could I face the cold New Year, and know
I was not confident that you would go
  Far over ways that will be cold and drear
  Ere summer with her roses reappear ?
I did not mean to doubt.   There, now I know,—
Come ! o'er the New Year's white paths let us go.

New Year's Eve.

(36)

A LETTER.

THE words for weary weeks denied my heart,
   When 't last they came, an aching void supplied
   With joy that seemed too great, until it tried
To fill my eyes with crystal drops that start
When long-missed hands a kind caress impart
   To one whose soul some tenderness in vain
   Has yearned by night and day to know again,
In anguish past the reach of mortal art.

I think if once thou could'st but see my face
   Glow, lit with gladness that your letters bring,
Then see the crimson tide to joy give place,—
   Deep, quiet joy for such a simple thing
As seems to thee the letter thou dost trace,—
   Each day thou'dst make the heart that loves thee sing.

(37)

WHICH?

Or I am richer for the sight of thee,
  Which Fortune late, in bounteous mood, bestowed,
  Or I was richer while within abode
The cherished hope that I thy face might see.
To think that we would meet was ecstasy ;
  But, oh ! to know we met, to know we trod
  The self-same paths,—that, clasping hands, we rode
    Through purple shades, along nepenthean ways,
To haunts of peace and tender fantasy,—
    That, drifting with the idly drifting days,
  We looked our souls into each other's eyes,
  And dreamed the blissful dreams of Paradise,—
All this to know the richer maketh me,
For what hath been than what I hoped would be.

(38)

XXXVIII.

YOUR BIRTHDAY.

As soon as I unclosed my eyes to-day,
I drew my curtains hastily aside—
No one was near to hear me—and I cried,
" My darling ! " so intensely, though you lay
Far from my side, a thousand miles away,
In dreams, you must have turned to me and sighed.
The glorious sun was rising, and I tried
To watch him fringe with gold Dawn's robe of gray;
I hid his face, as children, with one hand,
And for a while was able, till he grew
So powerful he ruled the entire land ;
And wheresoe'er the king his glances threw,
A glory was. A love I thus hid, erst,
As gloriously on my life hath burst !

(39)

NIGHT BY THE SEA.

BELOVED, my Belovëd, earth would be
  So sweet that heaven itself would be forgot
  If you and I might linger in this spot,
Might live and die together by the sea,
Where we have learned to love so deathlessly;
  That, whatsoe'er the griefs Fate may allot,
  Not death itself from my glad soul can blot
Remembrance of the joy you've yielded me.

That little boat we watched an hour ago
  · From darkness steal out to that silver path
That seems to lead to heaven, we both do know
  Must pass through midnight shadows, now it hath
So happy lingered in that light : nor we
Can heaven have now and in eternity !

XL.

PAWNS.

I.

A RING.

A HEAVY band of gold, within it set
  A diamond, whose every glance betrays
  Perfection, while I, fascinated, gaze.
Proud princess among jewels! doth regret
Ne'er stir thy white heart's depths? Canst thou forget
  The snowy hand thou'st graced in other days,
  As Night a tear-drop on the lily lays?
What tender, tremulous hopes thou didst beget
In some fair woman's breast!

                        Ah, I believe
Thy history, if known, would win a tear.
  O'er losing thee, it must be, two hearts grieve;
Surely 'twas Poverty who dragged thee here,—
  Estrangement, Pride, nor Death would ever show
To careless eyes: " My Darling " traced below.

PAWNS.

II.

AN OPERA-CLOAK.

It might have been a queen's, this lovely thing,
  Of purple and soft, creamy satin made.
  The breath of some luxurious beauty swayed
This down, as white as any angel's wing.
It may have been while she was suffering,
  And very weary of the part she played,
  Her heart away with her dead lover laid,
While still she strove to lightly laugh and sing. . . .
  I wonder if it ever has belonged
  To one who deemed herself too deeply wronged
To rise again? who may have felt a sting
Beneath this down, because so like the wing
Of some fair angel,—what she might have been,
And what she may be now,—for all her sin?

(42)

A LITTLE LETTER.

Love ! how the lone hours drag when you are far !
Life rushes onward so when you are near !
The face of Pleasure now is blanched by Fear
Since I can never know just how you are.
Oh ! I should be more grateful that no bar
More cruel than an ocean parts us, Dear,
For am I not with you ? and you are here—
I have you as the evening has her star.

This is a lonely night, and all the day
Was lonely, Love !   I tried for your dear sake
To hide from you how hard my heart did ache.
Yet—were you sorrowing I would have you say
Only the truth—'twould make my sad heart light.
God bless you, guide you, guard you, Love—good-
    night.

SONNET.

Low leans the lily to the wooing breeze,
  See how she trembles 'neath his warm caress,
Yet, all unused to love, she strives to please,
  And, if she please, is filled with happiness.
Far other is the mien of yonder rose,
  Yclad is she with scornful majesty ;
Oh ! who shall dare his love to her disclose,
  Or haply keep unawed beneath her eye ?
E'en so 'tis vain to woo that heart of thine,
E'en so 'tis vain to worship at its shrine,
  Where sits enthroned high thought of things above,
Abstract, and noting not this verse of mine,
  Whose sober plaint must unavailing prove,
  E'en though it hide thy name as doth my heart thy love.

SONNET.

As one who in the anguish of the year
  (When nature stricken lies, and self-confessed)
  Withdraws himself and all his heart's unrest
Apart from haunts of men, to wander near
The reedy marge of some unruffled mere,
    And there uplifts his soul in prayerful quest
    Of Peace, whose after-coming makes him blest;

So, when emerging from their shades, I see
    The horrid shapes that prey upon my soul,
On wings of instant thought I fly to thee,
And in the shelter of thy sympathy
    Grow brave and strong to reassert control :
Then say, though actual presence be denied,
What fate shall here our kindred souls divide ?

(45)

FORGIVENESS.

NOT of thine own sweet nature could it be
That thou should'st thus betray me! Let me think
Thy dear lips, unaware, did careless drink
From some spring poisoned by mine enemy ;
Whilst thou, thy senses dulled by lethargy,
Dreamed not the draught would straightway make me
    sink .
So deep down in Despair's grave that the link
'Tween Death and Life were quickly snapped in me.

With prayer unceasing will I beg of God
To lift from off thy soul that cruel clod
The hand of Jealousy did place thereon.
To me—'tis death : this massive rock upon
A heart too stunned and bruised to feel again
Aught in thy once too tender touch save pain.

ESTRANGED.

I.

Do you think, dear Love, if we had known
That, ere another year had flown,
We should have drifted far apart,
We who for years claspt heart to heart,
Do you think we had been more tender ?

II.

Ah ! to think this is your natal day,
And I so near, yet miles away !
Why, I could reach you in one short hour,
Yet dare not send you even a flower,
Not even forget-me-nots !

III.

And I used to know your heart so well
That I could look in your eyes and tell

All that was there ; but now, to-day,
If we should meet, you would turn away,
Nor let me see your eyes.

IV.

Oh ! if you'd look just once again,
What should I find there, hate or pain,
Love or longing, or coldness, Dear,
Or—how my heart leaps to dream it—a tear
Calling me back again ?

A JUNE DAY IN NOVEMBER.

I.

THE wondrous fairness of the day
Is dying, Sweet, for aye, for aye,—

II.

Dying, and we cannot keep it here
For all your pleading look or tear.

III.

The glory fades from shore and river,
And we grow still.   Your dear lips quiver ;

IV.

As many thoughts as there'll be stars
Are there behind the crimson bars,

(49)

V.

Longing for words to set them free
Ere darkness hides your face from me.

VI.

How strange that June should come again,
And bring such joy, then leave such pain

VII.

Now as she dies, and bleak November
Creeps back again.   I shall remember

VIII.

As long as life with me shall stay
The beauty of this summer day.

IX.

I oft shall see as I see now
The fairness of your low, sweet brow,

X.

Your soulful eyes, your golden hair,—
The dying sunlight lingering there,

XI.

Making a halo 'round your head,—
And, oh, your mouth so richly red!

XII.

Your image in the water there
Is going with the light; the air

XIII.

Is chilly, Sweet; we cannot stay
Dreaming forever, though our day

XIV.

Was fair, and sad, and sweet—all three—
To you, my Loved One and to me.

XV.

The stars are up, the night comes fast.
Our day is dead,—forever past!

WITH VIOLETS.

I.

THE violets that I send to you
  Will close their blue eyes on your breast.
I shall not be there, Sweet, to see,
  Yet do I know my flowers will rest
  Within that chaste, white nest.

II.

O little flowers, she'll welcome you
  So tenderly, so warmly!   Go :
I know where you will die to-night,
  But you can never, never know
  The bliss of dying so!

III.

If you could speak!   Yet she will know
  What made your faces wet, although
I fain would follow you and tell her.
  There, go, and die, yet never know
  To what a heaven you go !

52)

A LAMENT.

" Sleep sweetly, Tender Heart, in peace."

TENNYSON.

I.

SPRING again, and fair, calm skies,
    Pearl and blue,
Yet in vain my aching eyes
    Search for you.

II.

From long dreamings wake again
    Spring's sweet flowers,
In my soul an infinite pain
    Which the hours

III.

Nor the years can take away ;
    Only tears,
Springing at the close of day ;
    When one hears

IV.

God's voice nearer in the calms
  Twilight brings,
Losing sight of day's alarms,
  Bitter stings.

V.

Spring again ! The second born
  Since that day
God called you, and left forlorn
  Me for aye.

VI.

Were you watching ? Do you know,
  Little One,
Whose hand brushed away the snow
  (Winter gone)

VII.

From your grave a month ago,
  From the cross
Mutely telling as years go
  Of my loss ?

VIII.

Have you heard me when I've said
    Prayers for you ?
Have you felt me when I've laid
    Flowers on you?

IX.

Nevermore shall spring return
    With her flowers,
That I shall not for you yearn ;
    And when lowers

X.

Autumn, with its frosts that kill
    Summer's flowers,
I shall want my Darling still
    At all hours.

March 13th, 1879.

AFTER.

" Love's too precious to be lost,
A little grain shall not be spilt."
IN MEMORIAM.

I.

" I'M sorry, and I hurried back
To tell you so," a sweet voice said ;
But I was wounded then, and pride
Forbade me e'en to turn my head.

II.

To-night I grieve and pray beside
Her grave, yet cannot shed a tear ;
Death parted us ere I could say
The words which now she cannot hear.

(56)

III.

I know, I know she pardoned me,—
  She was so gentle with me ever,—
Yet, all the same, wet, wistful eyes
  Do follow me, and will forever !

A WHITE ROSE.

" I wore this rose at my throat last night."

I.

THE white rose came, nor is it yet quite dead,
But, oh ! so near.   Its dying breath is rife
With 'wildering fragrance ; though you had not said
Your lips had touched it, I had known its life
Was thus prolonged by you.

II.

The rose was faithful, it has brought to me
The sign of your remembrance from afar
Before its death.   If I might this night see
The eyes this fair rose charmed, the lips that are
Quivering to meet my own !

(58)

III.

But, as I cry out this, the Morn steals near,
　Her blushes tinge the white face of my rose;
Is it from Morn's eyes or my own the tear
　That scorches our poor dying rose? God knows,
　And I, O dearest Heart.

GOOD-BY.

I.

ALL is still, the stars are fading
    From the early morning sky.
I am kneeling here persuading
    My poor heart that our good-by
Was not, after all, forever ;
Distance, days, nor death can sever
Soul from soul, though I may never
    See thy face again.

II.

I shall pass thy window, Dearest,
    As I take my life's new way ;
I shall fancy that thou hearest
    All my aching heart would say,
As I hasten on and leave thee
Lying there with naught to grieve thee,
Though this heart would fain believe thee
    Moaning in thy dreams.

(60)

III.

No ! I cannot hurry on ;
　Just one moment I must stand
In the snow there, ere the Dawn
　Takes her rose-light from the land.
Thou wilt hear my poor heart beating,
Feel that I am there entreating
God to guard thee till our meeting ;
　Now I rise and go !

HER LAST WISH.

CAMILLE.

I.

MARIE DUPLESSIS, a woman, well throughout all Paris
known,
Marie Duplessis lies grieving in her sumptuous home
alone.

II.

Save a famous grave-faced surgeon, save one maid whom
she can trust,
No one stands within that chamber save one visitor
august.

III.

Death has come here! Death has found her! Death, the
only one she fears,
He has found her now, and horror chills her poor soul as
he nears.

(62)

IV.

Now and then in her delirium, meek as any little child,
She will look up in their faces, and her own seems unde-
filed,

V.

Innocent, and, oh, how lovely! all her wealth of yellow
hair
Falling 'round her as a glory, now no longer as a snare.

VI.

Now the carmine lips, **that tempted** other souls till they
were lost,
Only part for moans, not kisses,—restlessly the head is
tost.

VII.

Nothing they suggest desiring, wearily she moans and
moans;
Ah! that voice, that voice so famous for its rich and well-
trained tones!

VIII.

Sweet, sweet voice, now so pathetic that the eyes of man
and maid
Moisten as they stand and wonder whither now her mind
has strayed.

IX.

Leaning o'er her now, the woman, loyal to her all these
years,
Hears her murmur indistinctly, sees her eyelids wet with
tears.

X.

Suddenly the blue eyes open! Reason has come back
again,
And the man of skill, perplexëd, her great want to find is
fain.

XI.

"Marie Duplessis, what is it? Name this hunger of the
heart,
For your wish's swift fulfilling I. if need be. will depart.

XII.

" Tell me ! "   Slowly turned the great eyes that had lured
    men's souls away
On the man,—" I want my mother, and she is so far away.

XIII.

" Far in one way.   I chose rather all these years to give
    no sign
That I lived, for, oh ! I could not let her white life come
    near mine !

XIV.

" Bring her here before delirium leads my mind away again ;
Punishment for me, the sinner, will begin to see her pain."

*   *   *   *   *   *   *

XV.

Swift into the peaceful country sped a messenger away,
Long indeed the sufferer deemed it until sunset the third
    day.

XVI.

When within that room, luxurious, poured the sunlight on
    that day,
Glided in a little figure,—knelt the peasant mother to pray.

XVII.

Kissed in the old way the white face, once, twice, thrice—
    then down beside
Her poor wanderer knelt the mother,—sobbed, and prayed
    'till Marie died.

SYMPATHY.

I.

Yearneth thy heart for a sweet friend dead,
Sigheth thy heart for a dear day fled?
    I pity thee, my friend.

II.

Hast known regret for a word unspoken,
When a loving heart did await some token?
    My friend, God comfort thee.

III.

Hast spoken ungently to one now gone,
Hast lain on her grave and grieved alone?
    I know God heard thy prayer.

(67)

IV.

Hast been harshly judged, misunderstood,
By one to whom thou'st wished but good ?
God understood thy heart.

V.

Has the friend of thy heart and soul false proved,
The friend of all the world best loved ?
Christ pities thee, poor one!

DISAPPOINTMENT.

" My heart and life flowed onward—deathward—
Through this dream of thee."

E. B. B.

I.

How much I thought of meeting you again !
   In watching for the joy that hour would bring
I lost what grace the past year brought to me,
   And, save the lesson, gained not anything.

II.

My heart was warm wrapped in its love for you,
   My memory blind to every face save one ;
I could not, had I died, more faithful been.
   The hour came and passed,—Love's time is gone.

III.

So warm to one, and to all others cold,
   Selfish to all, yet generous unto you ;
Saving my eyes, voice, lips, as I had sworn,
   Only too proud to prove my love was true.

(69)

IV.

Spring, erst so dear, brought violets in vain.
  " Spring will return," I said, and let them fade
Ungathered, for the first time in my life ;
    From one great hope not for an hour thought strayed.

V.

Fair June, rose-laden, raised her blushing face,
  And crept up to my very window-sill,
While I, who loved her so in years agone,
    Forgot to smile down on her there until

VI.

Fierce suns had kissed the color from her lips.
  And thus my year went by, the year I thought
Would be my brightest.   Now I have no wish
    To know what this New Year for me has brought.

A LULLABY.

.

I.

FALLS the snow, falls the snow,
  Softly at eventide,
Just as the angels come and go,
  Silent and white when down beside
Baby's bed they lean them low,
  Falls the snow, 'tis eventide.

II.

Snowdrop mine, snowdrop mine,
  Falling asleep like the flowers,—
Mine, mine, my baby, mine,—
  Safe while the chilly night lowers.
Sleep till the smiles of the angels shine
  Into your eyes as the sun in the flowers'.

SONG.

I.

COME, for the sun is going down,
　Evening without thee will be drear ;
Sleepless, my eyes still watch for thee ;
　Can'st thou my lone heart's plaint not hear ?
Dead in my bosom lie the flowers
　That you at parting gave to me ;
They ne'er again, nor our dead hours,
　Can live but in our memory.

II.

Could I but know, ere twilight fades,
　Whether thy heart were light or sad,
Then, though so far away from thee,
　I could, like thee, be sad or glad.
But darkness falls, I cannot see thee,

Longing, I call on thee in vain,
Not e'en to know, while night comes down,
    Whether we e'er shall meet again ;
Oh ! when my life, like daylight, fades away,
    Must I, my Darling, call for thee in vain ?

MY LOVERS.

" The loneliness of life
Because I miss thee, Love!"

I.

NEXT to the children in the green square,
And their innocent laughter on the air,
Is the loveliness of my neighbor's face,
And her womanly, winsome, ineffable grace
As she leans to list for her lover.

II.

And next to all this is her Lover brave,
Who cannot look stern, e'en his life to save,
From the moment he rushes, that corner around,
Till he reaches his Sweetheart's door with a bound—
When I miss her fair face from the window.

(74)

III.

That Lover is no more afraid to show
His great heart in his eyes, and to let the world know,
  Than a baby to turn to his Mother, and call
  Her dear names, and to kiss her : and this, after all,
Is the very best kind of a Lover !

IV.

I could tell you, exactly, the steps that he takes
From the corner there ; how—meanwhile—he makes
  A nice calculation how long it will be.
  How he flings back his bonny brave head to see
If she's watching for him at her casement !

V.

When I see them together, an aching regret,
Never envy—God knows—makes me long to forget. . . .
  Why ! They look as if nothing—no one—save Death—
Could dare now to part them. They blend like the breath
Of my violets here, and my sweet mignonette.

VI.

Last night I was restless. 'Twas lonely up here
In this room, solitary . . . A voice brave and clear,
　In the moonlight was singing a tender love-song.
　'Twas the voice of this Lover. Oh ! how I did long
" For the sound of a voice that is still."

VII.

They told me that little song died years ago—
" A dead failure," they wrote me. A failure ? Ah, no.
　If it drew these two closer, then not all in vain
　Was it written, thank God,—and though late comes my
　　gain,
It means far more than money to me.

VIII.

Sometimes when I watch them I have a good cry.
I long for the courage to say ere I die :
　" It was I, in my happy past, I wrote that song
　Which you sing with such meaning, that some nights I
　　long
To come in, for a moment. I've wished you both knew
How, each night of my life—loveless—I pray for you."

HER EXPIATION.

" And lay the gift where nothing hindereth."

E. B. B.

THE hungry years can never be forgotten,—
    Those starved, long, lonely years apart from thee
Who wert my breath, my life, my only heaven.
    To-night, at last, I have crept back to see
Where they have laid all that is left of me,—
    For I am buried here.

                            In my despair,
I lie upon thy grave.   God cannot care
That I at last have sought thee.   I am Prayer
Incarnate, else, O Love! I would not dare
Here at thy feet my weary head to rest,
Nor lay this drenched, white lily on thy breast.

(77)

WASTE.

To one he sent his strong man's heart laid bare,
Quivering with hope and fear.   A cruel hand
Seemed pressing hard upon a hot, torn nerve.
Unto another faithless,—to her, true—
Nothing he kept, not even his fierce pride :
Complete surrender of his heart and life.

The second letter was indifferent—
Save for an old-time name he knew she loved.
He snatched a fading flower from his coat,
And crushed its purple blood against the words,
That she might know—for all his city life—
He still recalled her love for violets.

The one to whom he wrote with lashes wet—
His pleading was so strong and passionate—
Read, with fine scorn, his letter—flung it by,
And, later, answered—in a mocking tone. . . . . .
The other died.   Upon her broken heart
   Was found a locket with his face inside,
A tender name cut from a letter, and——a violet.

A PRAYER.

TEACH me to sing when my heart is aching,
  When my flesh is wounded, then let me laugh ;
Send me to comfort hearts that are breaking,
  Make me smile bravely when gall I quaff.

Send me with faith to souls that doubt Thee,
  Earnestness, deep, to the careless heart ;
Unto proud souls that have lived without Thee,
  Let me humility's grace impart.

Let me awaken those that slumber,
  Teach them to watch with fidelity ;
Place in my pathway thorns without number
  So I may lead but one soul unto Thee !

Let me be heedless of human praises,
  Let me be calm when dangers arise.
Let me gaze coldly where Passion blazes,
  Let me walk chastely, with lowered eyes.

(79)

Let me depart from my best and my dearest,
If by my staying I cloud a white thought :
Oft soul to the soul it loves best is nearest,
When lives, divided, with pain are fraught !

COMPENSATION.

" Let the world go by. Thou lovest me."

" HE cannot see." A kind voice said it low.
But, swiftly, one who led him closer leaned,
As though with life itself she would have screened
Her Lover's heart from e'en so light a blow.

He cannot see. But oh ! he feels her hand,
Charged with the love that fills her to the brim.
Her touch is sight and warmth and voice to him,
And his glad heart that light that ne'er on land
Nor yet upon the sea was ever seen—
(It hides in happy lover-hearts I ween)—
                        Is flooding now !

IN MEDITATION.

" *Who hides a sin is like a hunter who*
Once warmed a frozen adder with his breath,
And when he placed it next his heart it flew
With poisoned fangs and stung that heart
to death."

J. B. O'R.

BETWEEN the pages of this ancient missal rare,
A leaf was shut to mark a favorite passage there.
That one small leaf the priceless page did all corrode
As years rolled on,— 'twas left forgotten there: sad bode
Of how one secret sin may eat the priceless soul,
And then—eternal dole !

THE "LOOKING-GLASSES."

I.

THREE death-still pools in a lonely vale.
Still ! and so deep, so runneth the tale—
 No man hath been able their depths to sound,
 No mortal in all the fair country around—
  God's secret are they, I ween.

II.

And up on the hill, not far away,
The dead are lying, still as they ;
 The dead—whose bodies are in the ground,
 Whose souls are in deeps we may not sound
  'Till the sea gives up her dead.

III.

The sun shines warm on the gravestones white
This fair June morning. Look ! the light
 Lends to the black pools' surface a grace :
 Like a happy smile on a dead man's face,
  Whose soul may be lost forever !

BELGRADE.

(83)

TO THEE.

"My heart is lighted at thine eyes!"

I.

THY face is as the face of one
  Expectant—ready—if the morrow
Should summon thee henceforth to lie
        Within the arms of Sorrow.

II.

Thine eyes are listening when they're gray,
  Thou smilest—they are blue ;
And lo ! they are forget-me-nots
        That are agleam with dew !

III.

Thy voice !   It is as though thou wert
  Thy life's sole lover leaving—
A harp, whose strings the west winds kiss,
  And leave, at twilight, grieving.

(84)

IV.

A mouth so sweet and tremulous
  Mine eyes have never seen;
A tender word from thee must be
  Sweeter than Music's voice, I ween.

HER VOICE.

" And can'st thou think, and bear
To let thy music drop here unaware
In folds of golden fulness at my door?"

E. B. B.

Soft as to earth the snowflakes' fall,
Tender as names young mothers say;
Sweet as the secrets lovers recall ;
Earnest as prayers the angels pray
For souls astray.

Mournful as winds that wail at night
Around lone, ruined castle halls ;
Sad as the voice when lips are white
That vainly on its dear dead calls
When twilight falls.
Tearful as eyes just losing sight
Of Love, estranged forever.

(86)

BEYOND REACH.

" *A woman poor or rich,*
Despised or honored, is a human soul :
And what her soul is,—that, she is herself,
Although she should be spit upon of men
As is the pavement of the churches here,
Still good enough to pray in."

Aurora Leigh.

You know naught of the beauteous opal colors
Which Dawn and Sunset paint far on the summit
Of white-crowned heights no mortal e'er shall scale ;
You know not what the ocean may conceal
Far down beyond the reach of any plummet.
That woman whom you speak of with no mercy,
Whose spirit for your vision soars too high,
In deeps of silence hides such charities,
That God must fathom them—not you—not I.

AN INVALID.

HERS was the saddest face I e'er had seen.
Disease had gnawed her fair life to its core—
Nor yet fierce Pain could win sweet Patience o'er.
Just once I caught her radiant, rare smile : ·
A blush-rose blooming by a lone tomb door !

A MODERN PHILOSOPHER.

" Far better in its place the lowliest bird
   Should sing aright to Him the lowliest song,
Than that a Seraph strayed should take the word
   And sing His glory wrong ! "
JEAN INGELOW.

HE was a king to the adoring crowd
   That, wondering, hung upon his lightest word.
With human adulation he grew proud,
   And cried aloud—e'en little children heard—
"There is no God, no Heaven, and no Hell !"
   The eyes of innocent listeners opened wide.
Scandal to them ! That was the swift death-knell
   Of his fine mind—its powers all misapplied.
The words like wild-fire ran throughout the land :
   They never were recalled—it was too late.
That maniac there who bites his keeper's hand,
   And glares upon us through the iron gate—
Is he.

(89)

INDIAN SUMMER.

We saw the happy robins build their nests,
We watched the apple-blossoms bloom and fall,
Together knelt and searched for violets ;
Counted the petals of the marguerite,
Kissed each a rose, then wore it on his heart
Always together, each the other's world.

Sweet Summer flung herself on Autumn's breast,
Tired and flushed, her cheeks incarnadined,
At thought of having all unrobed to stand
Before a world, while Winter wove a shroud
For her—who never could come back to us,
For her—who brought such gifts to you and me.

With tenderness we said good-by to her—
Then heard the sweeping, equinoctial winds,
Singing, three days and nights, her requiem.

(90)

O Love! that wail was not for Summer, dead,
But for us two who unclasped hands that night,
Who said such bitter words ere we did part,
That Summer, who remembered, left her grave,
And showed her face, as perfect as of yore,
Against the blackness of bleak Autumn's breast :
Like golden, amber beads that glow against
An ebon rosary in the hands of Death.

QUATRAINS:

AFTER THE STORM.

ALL night a giant wind did rage with awful power.
  Morning uplifts her lustrous lamp.   Lo, I discern
A mighty, granite fortress with a shattered tower,
  And, nodding in the breeze, unharmed, a baby fern.

TWO ACTORS.

He who evoked our heartfelt sympathy and sighs,
  The coppers from his benefactor's eyes did borrow.
He who could laugh the tears from even Grief's own eyes,
  Scarce ever raised his own sad face from breast of
    Sorrow.

TWO KINGS.

The great king's jester said one word too much,
  The finite king his foolish head did sever.
One who for years blasphemed an infinite King,
  Was doomed at last in hell to burn forever.

Wisdom versus Weakness.

" This scientist has roused the entire world
  By his discovery ! "   Reading which, I smiled,
Remembering how, a day or two before,
  He was confounded by his lisping child.

THE SURFACE AND THE DEPTHS.

NESTLING in rocks, high on a rugged mountain,
I found a tender fern, just half uncurled :
A grave, stern face that I had thought forbidding,
Flashed me the sunniest smile in all the world !

"ONCE, AND ONLY ONCE, AND FOR ONE ONLY."

BROWNING.

WITH fervor they all cried : " We envy you
  The gift of making such a perfect song !"
It saddened him. His lonely heart did long
  For praise—not of the world—not of the few—
            Of only One.

INSPIRATION.

" Kings have commanded nations for a little time ;
Artists command the ages."

BALZAC.

A LITTLE child with eager, rosy face,
  Sprang forward, flower-laden, raised her head.
Poised thus, a question in her lovely eyes,
  Sculpture an instant saw her ere she fled,
          And gave us—" Hope."

(95)

A MAN'S LAST CRY FROM THE VERGE.

IF we had parted that first night,
  Indifferent—light-hearted ;
Had I but fled your presence bright
  That first time that I started,
          Then lingered so,
          Dreading to go ;
Had not returned to try with you
That last waltz, and to vie with you
          In war of words—
          Both had been saved !

If we had spared each other then !
  We dared each other, you and I,
Meeting as would have met two men,
  Each having sworn the other shall die
          For storied wrong
          Which each has long

Sworn to avenge for his dead sire—
Sworn by his faith, though little ire
   Feels either, now they have met !

But parting now, Love ! Parting now.
 Never to know, yet wondering whether
(E'en though each shall keep his vow),
 We two e'er shall stand together
   Ere we die, Love,
   You and I, Love,
Bound by a thousand tender ties—
Who have seen ourselves in each other's eyes.

   Why—'tis tragedy
   Now to part.
 Yet would love perish
 Did we not cherish
   Honor and Loyalty.
Now it will live—
God will forgive.
   Pray for me, Love !

LE PRINTEMPS.

SINGING to leaning ferns, I hear a brook
Way down in mossy reaches out of sight :
I seem to catch the low laugh, not the look—
Of some fair nun behind her veil so white
                    Hiding her face.

PLEADING.

My friend—so loved,—estranged from me to-night,
  Estranged from me whose lonely heart is beating
For God and thee alone,—come, bless my sight !
  Over the hills and waves hear me entreating
God's peace between us two ere dawns the light
  Of that immortal day whereon Christ came
                     To heal all wounds.

It is not that I miss so much the light
  E'en of thy blessed presence.   Dear, my grief
Springs from a deeper source : that thou should'st fight
  Temptation, woe, and doubt that kills belief,
And disappointment's sorrows that do blight
  The hopes of heart and soul—
    When I could shield thee,
      In my arms enfold
        Thee, wounded, as of old.
      Come thou to me—
        Else call me unto thee !

PRESCIENCE.

I.

Two angry lovers—loving still each other—
　　Her cheeks aflame, white—e'en as death—his face.
One keen-edged word has clashed against another
　　'Till softly one departs.　The time of grace
Is past.　Down on her knees she sobs: " Dear God! Too
　　late."

II.

White sails are set.　Soft summer winds are sighing.
　　Light laughter clashes with the low farewell.
A sea of lifted faces.　He is trying
　　Never to see one face he loves too well.
Into her eyes, intense, her soul has leaped—too late.

III.

All days, all nights thereafter deepen sadness.
Tired her fevered brain forever thinking
　　Upon two broken lines.
　　　　　　　　One night comes Madness.
That hour a strong man sobs while he is sinking
　　Into his deep-sea grave: " Dear God! am I too late?"

(100)

AT THE END OF EXILE.

" I found happiness in wedding thy sufferings."

OF all the world, Belovëd, to think thou art not here—
Now, I am dying. Not thine the fault, I know—Dear
  Heart.
Take my last thought : all pain I've known for our love's
  sake,
Was joy, whose like the whole wide world could not
  impart !

HEART'S OWN.

" Dear one,—whose name I name not lest some tongue
Pronounce it roughly."—H. H.

I.

I KNOW a singer :
And when she stands before them all,
Smiles, and then sings,—in her sweet thrall
The great crowd sways.   None there may say :
" She sings to me ! "   One—far away—
Vibrates to every thrilling tone,
And she is his, and his alone.

II.

I know a painter :
Around him crowd great beauties rare,
With whom the World would ne'er compare
His Love—the loveliest of them all.
Her picture hangs not on his wall.
Within his soul 'tis veiled, and there
Uncovered, only with a prayer.

(102)

III.

I know a poet :
Out of his solitude and pain,
Spring songs whose sweetness brings a rain
Of tears from e'en the cold World's eyes.
He knows but one Love 'neath the skies,
And she, for long, sad years has lain—
Within her grave. She feels the rain—
That wild, sweet rain—her joy, her pain :
Her Lover's tears.

REPLETION.

"Heaven bless thee.
Thou hast the sweetest face I ever looked on."

THAT face of thine, that face of thine,
And all thy lovely self, Dear One,
When first thy dear eyes answered mine
Seemed perfect. "Oh! what have I done,"
(I asked God humbly) "that to me
Thou givest this human blessing rare?"
"My perfect flower!" I breathed o'er thee,
"God never fashioned flower more fair."
Then, when between thy dear lips stole
Thy voice in song—like lark's on wing—
I whispered to my happy soul:
"It is as though a rose should sing!"

RELINQUISHMENT.

And yet because I love thee, I obtain
From that same love this vindicating grace:
To live on still in love, and yet in vain—
To bless thee, yet renounce thee to thy face.

E. B. B.

IF but to have thee near me in a dream,
  Doth thrill me 'till Joy breaks the spell of Sleep,
  Doth so ineffably my spirit steep
In deep delight, that waking pleasures seem
As naught compared with that which is supreme;
  If I am satisfied the while I keep
  Just near thee in a dream, and, waking, weep;
Then to arise, and see thy face, I deem,
  Were happiness too great for me to bear.
  And so, 'twas kinder that thou wast not there.
  Dear! If the dream proved true I would not care
To ever leave thee; nor could I say nay
To thy pathetic pleading 'till the day
My soul were summoned hence,—Life flung away!

(105)

TOO LATE.

I.

WHAT now are laurels to me, oh, my lost Heart,—
  Nay, never lost—only waiting somewhere,
What do I care for the wreath on my brow, Love,
  Too late to lay it on thy waving hair.

II.

Oh! how we watched for the coming of Fame, Love,
  Always thy cheek laid to mine while we waited;
Always thy firm little hand warm in mine, Love,
  How, when she neared, thy sweet face grew elated!

III.

Honors come late to thy Lover. Thy hero,
  Losing that guidance, no longer is brave;
Stifled all yearnings for Fame's lonely heights, Love,
  This is my resting-place, this little grave.

(106)

GOOD-NIGHT.

Good-night, dear heart, so far from mine
Good-night, fair face, for which I pine,
O'er thy life's way forever shine
    God's radiant stars.

O golden head! O fair, proud face!
Unmatched in all the world for grace,
How far thou art from thine own place
    Upon my heart!

Though miles and miles do intervene,
Thine eyes, Dear One, and mine atween,
From Morn's birth till the death of E'en
    Mine watch for thee.

Good-night, dear lips and tender eyes,
Sweeter are none 'neath any skies,
Angels watch o'er thee 'till the dear eyes
    Unclose in heaven.

Farewell, fond heart, so far away ;
Oh ! for the power Thought owns,—to stay
Near thee forever, by night, by day ;
     Sweetheart, good-night !

THE END.

www.ingramcontent.com/pod-product-compliance
Lightning Source LLC
Chambersburg PA
CBHW032019010726
47493CB00007B/2477